BOOK ANALYSIS

Written by Aude Decelle
Translated by Carly Probert

AF131429

To Kill
a Mockingbird
BY NELL HARPER LEE

Bright
≡Summaries.com

NELL HARPER LEE

AMERICAN WRITER

- **Born in Alabama in 1926**
- **Died there in 2016**
- **Works:**
  - *To Kill a Mockingbird* (1960), novel
  - *Go Set a Watchman* (2015), novel

Born in 1926 in Alabama, Nell Harper Lee began studying law before going to live in New York, where she found a job working for an airline company and spent her free time writing. Published in 1960, *To Kill a Mockingbird* was an immediate success. Two years later, Robert Mulligan adapted the story into a film starring Gregory Peck. In 2015, Harper Lee's publisher released a sequel that Lee had written decades earlier, entitled *Go Set a Watchman*. However, it was met with great criticism and many readers are unsure that Lee ever intended for it to be published. It is now generally accepted as being a first draft of *To Kill a Mockingbird*, rather than a sequel.

TO KILL A MOCKINGBIRD

A CHILD'S VIEW ON THE SERIOUSNESS OF THE WORLD

- **Genre:** novel
- **Reference edition:** Lee, H. (2002) *To Kill a Mockingbird*. New York: HarperCollins.
- **First edition:** 1960
- **Themes:** childhood, racism, disillusionment, intolerance, legal trials

To Kill a Mockingbird was published in 1960 in North America, in the middle of the fight for black civil rights. After publication, the novel won the Pulitzer Prize in 1961 and has sold over thirty million copies worldwide. This novel of initiation tells the story of a few years in the life of Scout, a little 6-year-old girl, while her father, a lawyer, defends a black man who has been accused of raping a white woman.

Combining the lightness of childhood memories with the gravity of racism and ordinary stupidity, this story set in a small town in Alabama in the 1930s, at the time of the Great Depression, is wonderfully told from the naïve and often amusing perspective of young Scout.

SUMMARY

The story takes place in Maycomb, Alabama during the thirties. Scout and Jem Finch are two children aged 6 and 10 who live near a house that both intrigues them and terrifies them: the Radley house, home to a bizarre family that lives in recluse. During the holidays, they meet another child, Dill, who is staying with his aunt. The three children soon become friends. They play together and the following summer they invent a role play game based on the Radleys, despite Atticus, Scout and Jem's father, forbidding them to do so. One evening, the children venture onto the porch of the Radley house, when a shadowy figure appears and scares them away. A shot rings out. They run off, scared to death. On the way, Jem loses his pants. When they return, Dill invents a believable reason to explain his lost clothing.

In September, Scout starts school but is disappointed by her teacher, Miss Caroline, whose teaching methods are not suitable for the poor children of Maycomb. Scout, who has long been able to read and write, gets on the wrong side of her teacher and finds herself banned from reading, which is a terrible punishment for her as she loves to decipher the newspaper with her father. After this disappointing day, Scout does not want to go back to school. Her father offers her a compromise: she can continue to read the newspaper with him if she carries on going to school. She accepts. One day, on the way home, she finds some chewing gum hidden in a tree in front of the Radley yard. This happens a few more times. However, one morning Jem discovers, with great dismay, that the opening in the tree has been filled in with cement.

The winter arrives and brings snow, which is a rare occurrence in Maycomb: the school is closed for the day. Jem and Scout make their first snowman. In the night, Atticus wakes the children and brings them out into the street as the house next door is on fire. Without Scout noticing, Arthur Radley drapes a blanket around her shivering shoulders.

The children's father is a lawyer. He is officially appointed to defend Tom Robinson, a black man accused of raping a white woman. At school and in town, reactions to Atticus' actions are virulent and Scout ends up fighting a classmate who teases her about it. Their father tries to prepare for the upcoming trial and the consequences it will have for their family. On the way to town, Scout and Jem pass by the house of Mrs. Dubose, an elderly woman who is sick and bad-tempered, and she provokes them about the trial. Furious, Jem destroys her flowers. Atticus orders him to apologize for his actions. In return for forgiveness, Mrs. Dubose requests that Jem comes to read to her for a month. Therefore, the two children go to visit the old lady's house every day. After her death, they discover that their presence helped her to control her morphine addiction.

As Tom Robinson's trial draws nearer, the backlash against the family multiplies. One evening, sensing that things are getting worse, Atticus goes to guard the prison where Tom Robinson is being held. The children, curious as to why he is going out so late, go to find him. They witness a heated argument between Atticus and a group of farmers who came to lynch the prisoner. Although she doesn't understand the situation entirely, Scout manages to resolve the conflict with her ingenuity.

At Christmas, Uncle Jack pays them a visit and they then join Aunt Alexandra, a narrow-minded and critical woman. She has a young son of Scout's age: the two children argue about the trial.

As for Jem, he changes considerably: he grows up, isolates himself, and Scout understands him less and less. She learns that Dill would not be visiting this summer. However, one night, the two children discover the boy hidden under a bed: he ran away and has come to take refuge in their home. Atticus agrees that he can stay for a few days. Moreover, Aunt Alexandra comes to live with them in their home, but living together proves difficult and many fights break out.

On the day of the trial, the entire neighborhood seems to have turned up to watch. The children also attend and, discovering that there are no seats left, they are welcomed into the balcony reserved for blacks. The trial begins with the testimony of Bob Ewell, the father of the girl who says she was raped. The Ewells are among the poorest and most disliked people in the town. Atticus casts doubt on the fact that Mayella, the alleged victim, could have been hurt by the accused, who only has the use of one arm.

When Mayella is questioned, her confusing testimony betrays the misery of her living conditions, but she continues to accuse Tom Robinson of having raped and beaten her. Finally, Tom comes to the stand: he describes Mayella as a lonely girl who enticed him into her house and invented this story of rape after being rejected by Tom and her father walking in on her. Atticus defends Tom Robinson's version of events and highlights the role of racial prejudice in his case. Nevertheless, Tom is convicted, which comes as a huge shock to the children.

The next morning, Atticus is moved to discover that the black community has thanked him by leaving heaps of food on his porch. He goes into town, where Bob Ewell spits on him and threatens him. Later, Atticus returns from town where he found out that Tom Robinson has been killed for attempting to escape.

Alexandra organizes a tea party with the ladies of Maycomb. Scout is not pleased with this lady-like gathering that she doesn't understand at all. Impressed with her aunt, who faces the situation with humanity and courage, Scout changes her opinion of her – and of the fact of becoming a lady.

When school starts again, Jem, who has grown up, isolates himself a little more. Although less terrified by the Radley house, Scout remains nonetheless intrigued.

Moreover, things begin to return to normal for Atticus, with the exception of a few incidents with Bob Ewell. On Halloween, Scout is required to participate in a pageant dedicated to the history of the town, where the children are dressed up as food – Scout plays a ham. However, during the performance, she falls asleep backstage and is too late to enter. Embarrassed, she prefers to stay hidden in her ham costume to go home.

On the way, she and Jem are attacked. They are saved thanks to the intervention of Arthur Radley. When the sheriff arrives on the scene of the attack, he finds Bob Ewell stabbed to death. Everyone then understands that Bob Ewell had tried to kill the children. Atticus believes that it was Jem who killed Bob in self-defense. The sheriff explains to him that it was Arthur Radley who stabbed Bob Ewell, but it would be better if this remained a secret.

Scout accompanies Arthur Radley to his house. She imagines herself in his position, looking out onto the street where the two children play, her and her brother, and she looks back on the events of the past few months.

CHARACTER STUDY

SCOUT (JEAN LOUISE FINCH)

Jean Louise Finch, known as Scout, is the heroine and narrator of the book. She is 6 years old at the beginning of the story. A small and very lively girl, who is rather tomboyish (she isn't afraid to hit those who bother her), Scout is close to Jem, her older brother, with whom she has a very complicit relationship. She has friends, but none that are girls and, curiously, there is no other female character her age in the book.

She is a child who reflects on and analyzes the things around her: she asks the adults many questions, trying to understand and observe the enormous world around her. Scout is sometimes innocent and other times terribly lucid, and she doesn't always know how to decipher the adult world, which remains a constant source of perplexity to her. Her humorous outlook highlights the absurdities and contradictions of the rules established by society, but she also illustrates the egotistical and naïve side to childhood.

Impulsive and carefree at the beginning of the novel, she evolves more towards wisdom and maturity as the months pass and she is confronted with evil (racism, injustice). Her father guides her into a compromise between accepting the real world and respecting essential moral principles.

JEM (JEREMY FINCH)

Jem is Scout's brother and four years older than her, and he also changes as the story develops: he goes from a boy to a future young man. He assumes his role as a big brother perfectly, leading Scout in most of his adventures, sometimes protecting her, other times consoling her, and, most of all, acting as a great 'theorist of life': because he is older, he can explain to his little sister his perceptions of the world around them.

Unlike Scout, who didn't know her well, he remembers with great sadness their mother, who died several years ago, and is sometimes overcome with nostalgia.

DILL (CHARLES BAKER HARRIS)

Dill, the friend of Scout and Jem, is an orphan who comes to spend his summer holidays with their neighbor, Miss Rachel Haverford, who he calls his aunt. He is imaginative and always ready to invent incredible stories. He announces that he is engaged to Scout, which is manifested by his stolen kisses and some tender letters. His character was inspired by Truman Capote, who the author had known as a child.

ATTICUS FINCH

Atticus is the father of Scout and Jem. He is about fifty years old and a widower, and he brings up his children alone, according to principles that are rather liberal for his time. A lawyer, he takes the defense of Tom Robinson (falsely accused of raping a white woman) to heart, even though he knows that the trial is already lost.

Understanding with his children, he is very perceptive and knows how to balance fair severity with benevolent flexibility. The freedom with which he teaches them is not always approved in the small bigoted town in the Southern United States where he lives, and his sister blames him for educating Scout and Jem like savages – the biggest disgrace being that Scout is wearing overalls instead of pretty dresses like other girls her age.

CALPURNIA

Calpurnia, the Finchs' black cook, is like a member of the family and is involved in the upbringing of the children, who lost their mother when they were very young. She is also tough but fair, and she agrees with Atticus Finch on most of the educational and moral principles that are instilled into them. It was she who taught Scout to write, and she is one of the few people in the black community that can read.

AUNT ALEXANDRA

Aunt Alexandra, Atticus' sister, lives in a world of very strict principles and resents the way her brother is raising his children. She believes that she is allowed to intervene in their education and tries to make Scout a "proper" young person, forcing her to wear dresses and attend tea parties that she organizes with the ladies of Maycomb.

She is nonetheless loyal to Atticus, and she stands her

ground during and after the ordeal of Tom Robinson's trial, proving herself to be more humane that she first appears.

THE NEIGHBORHOOD

In this small town where everyone knows one another, neighborly relationships are rather narrow. Scout identifies the neighbors who are hostile or indifferent (Miss Stephanie Crawford, who is a curious and talkative gossip and never short of slanders) and those on whom she can rely, such as Miss Maudie Atkinson, a widow who is the same age as Atticus and has the same broad and noble ideas as him.

Among the nearby houses, the one that arouses the curiosity of the inhabitants of Maycomb in general, and the Finch children in particular, is that of the Radley family. The family is never seen and one of their sons, Arthur 'Boo' Radley, is suspected of committing the worst atrocities.

ANALYSIS

WRITING ABOUT CHILDHOOD: REALISM OR FALSEHOOD?

A story of childhood told by Scout, aged 6 at the beginning of the novel, aged 9 at the end, *To Kill a Mockingbird* presents a dual outlook: it is both naïve and terribly lucid, and sometimes verges on cynicism. Through this, the reader senses the presence of an adult who is writing about and taking advantage of this childish narrator to mix the sometimes simplistic analyses with the crudest of realities. Even when Scout is mistaken and her perception of the situation is skewed, the author intervenes with a lagging tone that points out the error of the young narrator. The resulting effect is mostly very comical and the tone of the novel is full of humor from start to finish.

The binary rhythm of the narration, with the opposition of the summer holidays/school term, highlights how the holidays represent tremendous freedom for a child. These are the times of games, discovery, learning, and growing up. The days sometimes seem to last forever, while the moments that happen at school, with the exception of Scout's first day which is thoroughly described, are virtually ignored and are subject to a systematic ellipse of time.

AN INITIATORY NOVEL: FROM BLISSFUL CHILDHOOD TO DISILLUSION

The two main protagonists, Scout and her brother Jem, grow

up in front of the reader and go from being naïve children to soon-to-be young people. Their evolution emerges from anecdote to anecdote – the novel also sometimes resembles a collection of stories that can be read independently of one another. Some are small, others are more serious. Each little story seems to be an opportunity for the children to learn a life lesson, discover a trait of human nature and, at the same time, get to know the other, and accept difference. Their father is a true guide who always appears fair and clairvoyant, and never shows negative or overly subjective emotions.

The reader specifically follows the evolution of Scout, since she is the narrator. As the story develops, she goes from disillusionment to disillusionment. She must first give up on her ideal school as she soon realizes that she won't learn anything useful at school. She also gradually learns to separate herself from her brother, who is growing up and sometimes needs to get away and thus break the complicit bond between them. By disassociating herself from him, she nonetheless learns to accept the idea of becoming a woman and gains a female role model, her aunt, who she finally recognizes as having some qualities.

The trial shows the three children how human justice is un-fair and imperfect, and portrays a world of men that seems harsh and cruel. The analysis that their father actually gives nonetheless leaves a place for hope and tolerance. Atticus Finch indeed finds the positives in a sea of disasters. Facing the unjust verdict of the jury, he explains to his children that by fighting to defend Tom Robinson, he still gained something: the case has been the subject of much delibe-ration, which is an improvement compared to all the cases where black men were automatically found guilty. In doing so, he comforts himself as he is extremely affected by the failure of the trial, even though he already knew what its outcome would be.

At the very end of the novel, after Bob Ewell's assault on the children, Scout realizes how all the events have made her and her brother older: "I thought Jem and I would get grown but there wasn't much else left for us to learn, except possibly algebra" (Chapter 31).

AN AVANT-GARDE EDUCATION

Throughout the novel, Atticus acts as a benchmark for Scout. Although he expects a lot of his daughter, he also respects her enormously and his love and his tender and understanding attitude help the girl stay on course.

Atticus treats his children with respect and speaks to them like adults, while recognizing their limits. So, faced with their questions, he does not lie to them and does not try to hide things from them. Instead, he tries to give them the right tools to make sense of the world and prepare them for the future. Even in the event of a conflict or a tough blow, he teaches his children to put themselves in the shoes of others rather than hating or despising them, and repeatedly tells them not to judge others.

Although he transmits a lot through education and dis-cussion, he also does so through the example he sets of an honest and deeply humane man, who doesn't hesitate to defend a lost cause because someone has to do it and he is strong enough to carry the burden. His character bears a slight similarity to Christ, entrusted by others to confront what they do not have the courage to face themselves and bearing the weight of the injustice of a flawed society; in this sense, the trial is his "Way of the Cross", with the ultimate failure of the verdict. But he transcends the test to which he finally gives a positive turn. He offers his children a lesson in courage and dignity, according to the logic of his character throughout the story.

In any case, he is a very modern father figure in the small rural town during the 1930s in the Southern United States.

RACISM AND INTOLERANCE IN RURAL AMERICA IN THE 1930S

Racism is the background topic of this story, with the trial of a black man, but segregation and rules governing relations between blacks and whites are also present throughout the novel. This corresponds to the reality of the time: both groups were living apart, and injustice and racism were common occurrences in the black community. It must not be forgotten that the first actions of Martin Luther King (American pastor and pacifist leader in the fight for civil rights, 1929-1968) against segregation did not take place until the sixties – when the novel was written.

In this regard, the Finch family goes against the society in which they live. Atticus treats everyone equally, whether they are black or white, rich or poor, educated or not. Calpurnia seems to be a part of the family and he doesn't object to Scout visiting her at her home in the black neighborhood, nor to his children attending mass and the church of the black community. Through his attitude, he is going against his contemporaries and must sometimes fight within his own family, for example, when his sister Alexandra suggests that he parts with his cook.

The racist attitude of most people in Maycomb Country refers to the general intolerance towards difference. Adults seem trapped by a network of principles and strict rules that dictate their conduct and govern their relationships. Thus, Mr. Dolphus Raymond, who married a black woman, pretends to be a drunk in order to be left in peace, his alcoholism being sufficient to justify his deviation in the eyes of the inhabitants. Bigotry and sectarianism, which are both features of the whites, characterize many rigid and often ridiculous characters, including Aunt Alexandra who is molded by unwavering principles on what is and isn't appropriate, with whom she can socialize, what clothes a woman should wear, etc. These traits particularly appear among the women: aside from Alexandra, Stephanie Crawford shows snide intolerance on her part, while Miss Caroline, Scout's first teacher, appears frankly displaced with her teaching methods that are unsuitable for the poor and rural area where she teaches.

Rural and urban settings, poverty and affluence are also part of the value system in this society where everyone occupies a specific grade, especially during this troubled period of the

Great Depression – a time marked by economic crisis, high unemployment and famine after the stock market crash of 1929, whose repercussions in Europe would later promote the ascension to power of Adolf Hitler. Thus, the barriers between classes are impassable and the few who dare to try will pay the full price, like Mayella Ewell, the girl who was allegedly raped by Tom Robinson.

FURTHER REFLECTION

SOME QUESTIONS TO THINK ABOUT...

- History, whether the history in school books (Civil War) or individual history (the Finch family tree), appears in the background of the story on many occasions: what does this mean with regards to the events that happen to Scout?
- Rites and conventions punctuate the lives of the inhabitants of Maycomb. Are they responsible for a form of torpor? Or do they represent a kind of handy barrier, allowing the inhabitants to overcome certain constraints?
- Examine how the female characters play an important role in the transmission of rules and identify their main characteristics. Are the positive female characters the most similar to the men?
- The black and white people coexist, but they know little about each other and live in two separate worlds. What are the moments in the novel where these worlds really cross?
- In what way is the trial like a show, almost like a play of human tragicomedy?
- The characters in the novel are almost never physically described; they are presented through their actions or their words. From this, can we identify lexical fields that define every major character?
- In your opinion, what made this work so successful?
- Compare the book with the film adaptation directed by Robert Mulligan. What differences do you notice?

We want to hear from you!
Leave a comment on your online library
and share your favourite books on social media!

FURTHER READING

REFERENCE EDITION

- Lee, H. (2002). *To Kill a Mockingbird.* New York: HarperCollins.

ADAPTATION

- *To Kill a Mockingbird.* (1962) [Film]. Robert Mulligan. Dir. USA: Universal Internation Pictures (UI).

MORE FROM BRIGHTSUMMARIES.COM

- Reading guide – *Go Set a Watchman* by Harper Lee

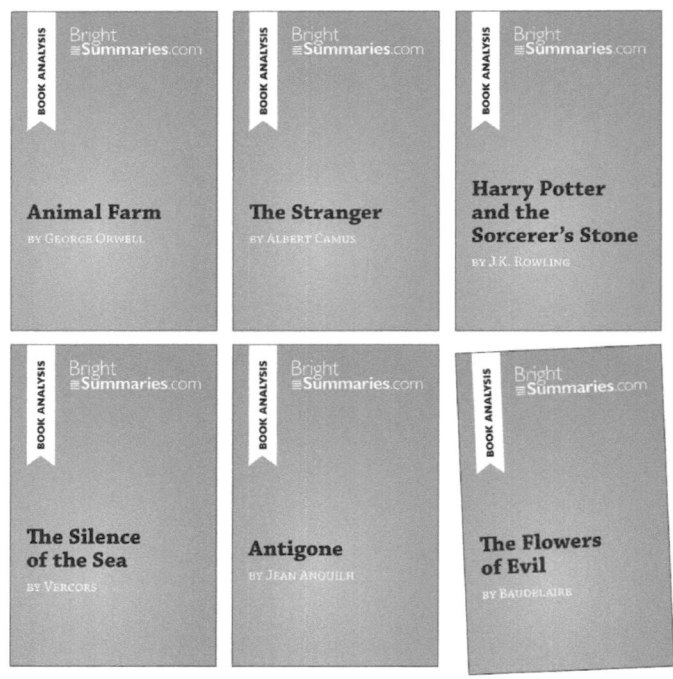

www.brightsummaries.com

Ebook EAN: 9782806270245

Paperback EAN: 9782806271624

Legal Deposit: D/2015/12603/509

Cover: © Primento

Digital conception by Primento, the digital partner of publishers.